JUDY MOODY AND FRIENDS

Amy Namey
in Ace Reporter

Megan McDonald
illustrated by Erwin Madrid
based on the characters
created by Peter H. Reynolds

CANDLEWICK PRESS

For Laura

M. M.

For my mom and dad,
Felicitas and Silvano Madrid

E. M.

Text copyright © 2014 by Megan McDonald
Illustrations copyright © 2014 by Peter H. Reynolds
Judy Moody font copyright © 2003 by Peter H. Reynolds

First edition 2014

Library of Congress Catalog Card Number 2013953452
ISBN 978-0-7636-5715-4 (hardcover)
ISBN 978-0-7636-7216-4 (paperback)

14 15 16 17 18 19 CCP 10 9 8 7 6 5 4 3 2 1

Printed in Shenzhen, Guangdong, China

This book was typeset in ITC Stone Informal.
The illustrations were created digitally.

Candlewick Press
99 Dover Street
Somerville, Massachusetts 02144

visit us at www.candlewick.com

CONTENTS

CHAPTER 1
Did King Tut Chew Gum? 1

CHAPTER 2
Taboo 25

CHAPTER 3
Above the Fold 47

CHAPTER 1
Did King Tut Chew Gum?

Amy Namey was looking for a story.
A big news story. A jump-off-the-page,
super-exciting story. She walked up
and down the street.

"This is Amy Namey, Ace Reporter,
on the beat."

She took notes in her notebook:

11:17 Mrs. Donovan's dog barked

11:22 Mrs. Donovan's cat chased Mrs. Donovan's dog

11:37 Rocky waved from upstairs window

11:39 Mrs. Moody got her mail

"Nothing ever happens in Frog Neck Lake," Amy muttered.

"Are you talking to yourself?" asked Judy Moody, kicking a soccer ball down the street.

"Hi, Judy. I'm being a reporter, and I need a big scoop."

"A big scoop?" Judy asked. "Let's go to Screamin' Mimi's! They have tons of scoops."

"Not the ice-cream kind of scoop. The *story* kind of scoop. A big scoop is an exciting story that nobody else knows about. It's for the newspaper I'm making. C'mon over to my house."

Judy and Amy kicked the ball back and forth all the way to Amy's house.

When they got there, Judy followed Amy upstairs to her room. Amy held up her newspaper for Judy to see.

"The Big Scoop," Judy read aloud. "Cool name."

Then Amy read the headlines to Judy. "There's a New Pig in Town. Frank Pearl Wins Blue Ribbon. Rocky Zang Learns New Card Trick. Judy Moody Does . . . something," Amy finished.

"Hey!" said Judy. "I do things! I went to college. And to Boston."

"I know! I'm not done yet," said Amy. She pointed to a big fat empty space on the front page.

"I'm saving the best story for last. Who knows? Maybe you'll be in it."

Amy's mom tapped on the door. "Hi there, Judy. Here are the papers you wanted, Ames," she said.

Amy spread the newspapers out all over her bed. "I asked my mom if I could read some of her news stories," Amy told Judy.

"*By E. Namey*," read Judy. "Wow. Is that you?" she asked Mrs. Namey.

"That's me," said Amy's mom. "A few of my biggest stories. See?" She pointed to the top of one paper. "If your story is on page one at the top, it's a big deal. That's called *above the fold.*"

DAILY NEWS SUN TIMES

FAMOUS BRIDGE MOVED TO VIRGINIA

"Neat-o," said Judy.

"I need something mega-exciting to put above the fold on *my* paper," said Amy. "Like this." Amy read a headline: "*Girl Finds 5,000-Year-Old Gum.*"

"Rare!" said Judy.

Amy chewed the end of her pencil. "Wait a second. Maybe *we* could find a way-old piece of gum, too, or something."

"Or something," said Judy.

"Then I could write about it."

"Double rare," said Judy.

"There's a story out there," said Amy. "And I'm going to sniff it out."

"I know just the place," said Judy. "Let's go!"

"Happy sniffing," said Mrs. Namey.

In no time, Amy and Judy were digging up the Moodys' backyard. Judy had a spoon. Amy had a bigger spoon.

Shoop! Shoop! Shoop!

Amy sifted through the dirt, looking for something way-super-old. "Just think," she said in a dreamy voice, "maybe we'll find a dinosaur bone."

"Or a shark tooth from a million years ago," said Judy.

"Or an arrowhead."

"Or an old-timey key. Or a super-duper-old coin from a way-long time ago."

"Yeah," said Amy, "like a penny that belonged to Abe Lincoln."

Amy looked at the pile of stuff they had dug up. "So far we found one marble, ten hundred rocks, one Donna Danger action figure, a rusty nail, an eraser, broken glass, a cherry pit, and three peanut shells."

"Maybe we found something old and don't even know it," said Judy, sifting through the pile. "Maybe your big scoop is right here under our noses."

Amy held up the marble. She rubbed off the dirt. "In ancient Egypt, King Tut, the Boy King, was buried with board games, right? This could be King Tut's marble."

Judy held up the eraser. "And this could be a caveman eraser. In case you make a mistake drawing your cave painting."

"Cavemen did NOT have erasers," said Amy, cracking up. "But maybe it's really a mammoth tooth. Or a dinosaur toenail?"

"Rare," said Judy. "What about this peanut shell?"

"I'm guessing . . . it could be . . . Abe Lincoln's," said Amy. "Just think—what if Abe Lincoln ate peanuts right here in *your* backyard?"

"That's a way-big-giant scoop," said Judy.

"Wait. What's this?"

Amy held up a dirt-covered lump. She blew on it.

It wasn't a nut. It wasn't a rock. It wasn't a ten-thousand-year-old cherry pit. It had teeth marks!

Amy's eyes grew wide.

Judy's eyes bugged out of her head. "Are you thinking what I'm thinking?" Judy asked.

"It's ABC gum!" said Amy. "Way-super-old, Already-Been-Chewed, Honest-to-Abe gum."

"It *looks* old," said Judy. "Did King Tut chew gum? Maybe it's three-thousand-year-old gum!"

Amy and Judy stared in awe at the way-old ABC gum.

"This is big," said Amy. "Really big."

Just then, Stink came running out the back door. He peered at the dirt-covered lump in Amy's hand. "Hey! My gum!" He snatched it and popped it into his mouth.

"Nooooooo!" Amy cried.

"Stink!" Judy shouted.

"What? It's not *that* gross," said Stink. "Just a little dirt. I was playing out here this morning and I lost my gum. I thought I swallowed it."

"There goes our three-thousand-year-old gum," said Judy.

"Hey!" said Stink, picking up the action figure. "Donna Danger! And my cat's-eye marble. And my eraser. Thanks, you guys. I thought I lost all this stuff."

"So all this stuff is Stink's?" said Amy. "Not King Tut's? Not Abe Lincoln's?"

"Sorry about your big scoop," Judy said.

"That's okay," said Amy. "I can always find King Tut's ABC gum tomorrow."

CHAPTER 2
Taboo

Amy Namey, Ace Reporter, was back on the beat. She waded ankle-deep in Frog Neck Creek behind her house.

This time, Amy Namey was monster hunting! Not the kind of monsters that live in books. Not the kind of monsters that live under the bed. The kind of monsters that live in lakes and rivers, creeks and streams.

Sea serpents! Like Nessie from Scotland!

Nabau from Borneo!

Nyami-Nyami from Africa!

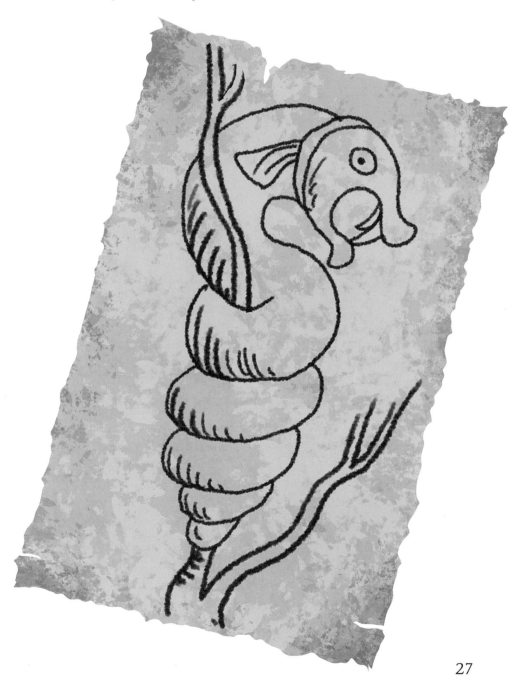

"This is Amy Namey, Ace Reporter and Monster Hunter, hot on the trail of the Great Virginia Sea Serpent. Will today be the day I capture the super-secret creature on film?"

Just then, something splashed behind her.

"Aaagh!" Amy's notebook went flying. She landed bottom-first in the creek.

"What are we looking for?" said a voice. A Judy Moody voice. Amy turned and saw Judy take a bite of the baloney sandwich she was carrying.

"Judy! You scared me! Never sneak up on a reporter who's sea-monster hunting."

"Sea-monster hunting!" said Judy. "Can I help?"

"Yes. If you give me your sandwich," said Amy. "I need bait."

"Sea monsters like baloney sandwiches?" Judy asked.

"Of course they do," said Amy.

Judy handed over the sandwich. "Too bad. It has double mustard and one whole dill pickle."

"It's for a good cause," said Amy. "My mom wrote a news story about this sea serpent named Nabau, in Borneo. So I'm looking for one, too. But they're hard to find. Almost nobody gets to see one."

Judy peered into the water. "Do they look like giant snakes?" she asked.

"Some do. Like Nessie in Scotland. And Cressie in Canada. And Bessie in Lake Erie. And Tessie in Lake Tahoe. And don't forget Ogopogo!"

"O-go-WHO-go?"

"Ogopogo. It's a lake monster. It lives in Canada, along with Cressie."

"Remind me never to move to Canada," said Judy.

"I'm looking for the Great *Virginia* Sea Serpent. His name is Taboo."

"Whoa," said Judy.

"Taboo has the long neck of a dinosaur, the fins of a shark, and the tail of a giant eel. And his eyes glow in the dark. See? I drew a picture."

"Freaky-deaky," said Judy.

Just then, Amy felt something slippery, something slimy, brush against the back of her leg.

"Aaagh!" she yelled. "My leg! I felt something! Taboo!"

"Was it slippery and slimy?" Judy asked.

"Yes!"

"Did it give you the creeps?"

"Yes!"

"It was just me." Judy held up a stick. "Hardee-har-har."

"You scared me so bad!" said Amy.

"Are you *sure* you want to find this thing? Sounds all creepy-crawly and swimmy-slimy to me." Judy shivered.

"How else am I going to be an Ace Reporter? First, I'm going to take a picture of Taboo. Then I'll write a story about it for my newspaper."

"Above the fold, right?" Judy asked.

Amy nodded. "Someday, I'll go around the world getting big scoops for the real newspaper. Like famous Around-the-World Reporter Nellie Bly. And my mom."

Just then, the two girls heard a giant, for-real splash. A NOT-Judy-Moody splash. They looked up the creek. They squinted into the sunlight. Water rippled over the rocks.

The two girls saw something bob up out of the water. It was riding the current. And it was heading downstream . . . right toward them!

"Do you see what I see?"

Amy gulped. "Yes. If what you see is a three-humped sea serpent with the head of a snake and the tail of an eel!"

"Do you think it smells my sandwich?" Judy asked.

But Amy wasn't listening. This was it! Her big scoop at last.

"I have to snap a picture," Amy said.

The two girls took a step closer. Amy snapped a picture. Something slippery brushed against her leg . . . *again.*

"Judy, stop touching my leg with that stick," she said.

"Stick? What stick?" said Judy. She held up both hands: empty.

Amy's heart went *thump-thump.*

"TA-BOO!" they both screamed.

They splished. They splashed. They slipped and slid.

They scrambled up the bank of the creek.

They ran across Amy's backyard.
They ran inside Amy's back door.

They ran into Amy's light, bright kitchen. "What's wrong?" asked her mom.

"Sea s-s-s-serpent!" said Amy, pointing to the creek.

"Big mon-s-s-ster!" said Judy, pointing out the back window.

"TABOO!" they both yelled.

"Phew. Close call," said Amy.

"Double phew," said Judy.

Amy held out her camera and zoomed in. She zoomed in closer.

"Hmm," her mom said. "It might be a big monster. Or it might be a big . . . imagination?"

"Mom, I saw it," said Amy.

"And don't forget we heard a big splash," said Judy.

"Girls," said Amy's mom, "do you think your sea monster just might be a three-humped tree branch?"

Amy shook her head.

"No way, no how," Judy said.

When Mrs. Namey left the kitchen, Amy turned to Judy. "This is big," she whispered. "Really big."

CHAPTER 3
Above the Fold

Amy Namey, Ace Reporter, took out the pencil from behind her ear. Amy took out her way-official notebook.

At last, she had a story. A real scoop.

Even famous Around-the-World Reporter Nellie Bly had never had a scoop this big. Nellie Bly had never spotted her very own sea monster.

Amy could not wait to write it down.

GREAT VIRGINIA SEA SERPENT SIGHTING
by Amy Namey, Ace Reporter

First there was Nessie. Then there was Nabau. Now there's Taboo. Did you know if you go monster hunting in Frog Neck Creek, you just might get mega-lucky and spot a sea monster? It's true.

Two girls from Virginia were out monster hunting this past Saturday in the Croaker Road area when they spotted something large and slimy in the creek. Eyewitness Judy Moody said, "It looked like a giant snake! No lie! It was SO not a tree branch."

If you plan to go sea-serpent hunting, take a good pair of rain boots. Need bait? Try a baloney sandwich.

And don't forget to take your camera.
Taboo, the Great Virginia Sea Serpent, was
captured on film. (See picture below.) Look closely.
Stick? Or sea monster? You decide.

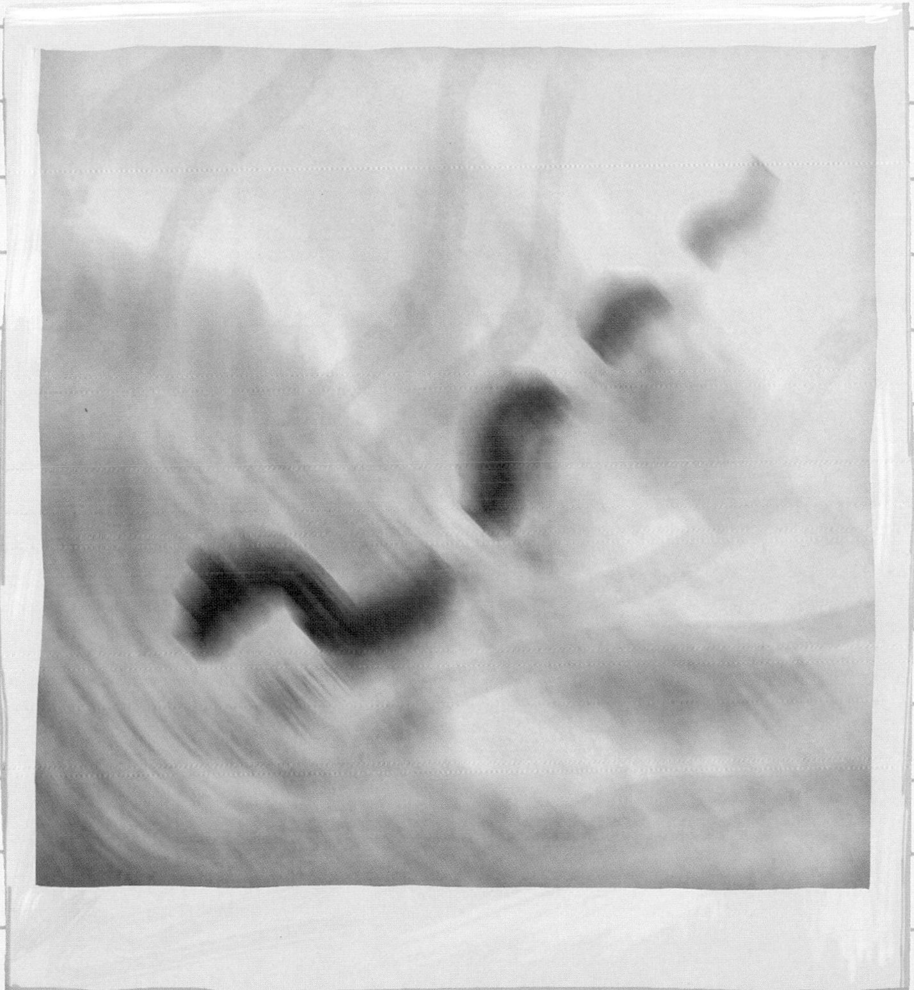

"Do you like my story?" she asked her mom, bouncing on her tiptoes.

"I love it," said her mom, giving her a squeeze. "It's exciting. It held my interest. And that ending is what we in the newspaper biz call a cliff-hanger."

"Wow," said Amy. "Thanks. Wait till I show Judy!"

Amy Namey, Ace Reporter, ran down the street to Judy's house. She showed the story to Judy. She told Judy all about cliff-hangers.

"This is the best front-page above-the-fold story *ever*," said Judy.

Amy ran back home to make copies for all of her friends. "Mom! Can you help me type up my story?"

"I'm up here!" called her mom. "In your room."

Amy ran upstairs. Something about
her room was different.

A desk! Her room had a desk! An old-timey rolltop desk, right in front of the window.

"Every writer needs a desk of her own," said Amy's mom. "This desk was mine when I was a girl."

"Really?"

"Yes. It's been collecting dust up in the attic forever," said her mom. "Do you like it?"

Amy closed her eyes. She smelled the old wood. She smelled the stories. She smelled the history.

"Are you kidding?" Amy hugged her mom. "I love it to pieces!"

Amy rolled back the top of the desk. Inside were little doors and secret drawers and cubbies.

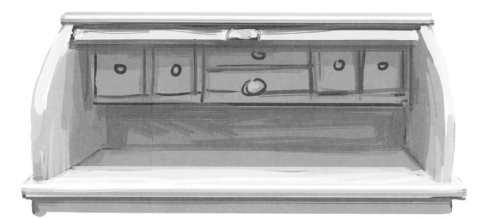

In one of the cubbies, Amy found a bunch of rolled-up papers.

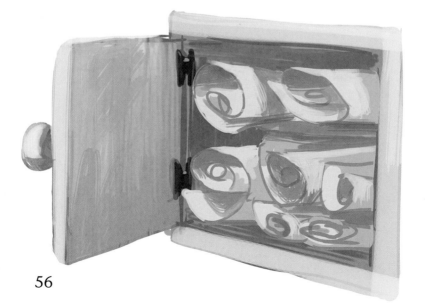

She pulled them out and unrolled them on the bed. *"The Tattle Tale,"* she read aloud.

"Oh, my old school newspapers!" said her mom. "These must be some of the first stories I ever wrote."

"Nice," said Amy.

"Here's a story I wrote about Fluffy the Rabbit, our class pet."

"Here's a poem called *Ladybug, Ladybug!*"

Together, Amy and her mother looked through all the old papers and laughed.

Later, after her mom had left
the room, Amy sat down at the old
wooden desk for the first time.

She pulled open a secret drawer.
She pulled open a tiny secret door.

Wait! Something caught Amy's eye.

Carved inside the door were some letters. Amy leaned in closer and touched each letter. They spelled a name: E-M-I-L-Y.

Her mother's name!

Amy picked up a pen. She carved three more letters into the wood, right next to her mother's: A-M-Y.

Amy was here.